Little Max's

Big

Adventure

Written and Illustrated By

Matt Gehring

Dedicated To Max

Hi! My name is Max, and I'm a dog! I go on adventures all the time when my owners take me with them on vacation, and I have met lots of funny animals on the way.

One summer, I found out we were going to Florida, and I got to go, too! The ride in the car was so long, but finally we were at the beach. That's when I found my first animal of my big adventure. As I ran through the sand toward the water, I saw a fish in the sea. His name was Eddy, and he told me that there was a lot to explore.

"Welcome to this giant sea,

I'm glad you came and talked with me!

If you want to go explore,

Then go now - be back by four!

Your family cannot find out

Don't tell them what your plan's about!"

-Eddy the Fish

I started walking back through the sand and I was soon on the grass. I saw a sign for a park, and figured that was a great place to go next. But I was not there yet, and still had a little bit of walking to do.

On my way to the park, I found a bunny sleeping on the grass. I was wondering what I could do once I was at the park, and thought that the bunny could probably help me out! At first, she was not very nice to me, but then she was very helpful.

"How dare you wake me from my sleep!

I was busy counting sheep!

Oh I think I slept too long,

Being mad at you is wrong.

The park is very, very fun,

Be sure to talk to everyone!"

-Laura the Bunny

After meeting the bunny, I continued toward the park, and soon enough, I was there. This was the biggest park I had ever been to! It was almost like a giant playground for kids and animals! On one side was a large, grassy area, and on the other side was a huge lake. All I kept thinking was that I couldn't wait to go swimming in it.

As I walked closer to the lake, I felt something zooming all around me. Usually when I feel this, it turns out to be the wind, but when I looked behind me this time, I saw a beautiful, blue butterfly.

"I'm a little butterfly!

All the time I flutter by!

I can fly upside down,

I fly all across this town!

Be sure to go visit the lake,

There are many friends to make!

-Meg the Butterfly

I wondered what she meant when she said I could make some friends. Maybe there were animals by the lake! Excited, I ran to the big lake to see what I would be able to find.

To start off, I was going to dive into the lake and have a swim. After that, I would look around for some more animals. But what happened next turned out to be my favorite memory from my adventure!

I was next to the lake and about to jump in when suddenly, a frog jumped up right in front of me! I fell over because he scared me so much, but I did laugh since it was kind of funny. Once my laughter stopped, we talked and became friends.

"Sorry if I just scared you!

I scared a dog earlier, too!

Maybe it's because I'm green,

In the grass I'm never seen!

Want to join me for a swim?

Oh, by the way, my name is Tim!"

-Tim the Frog

We raced all the way across the river, and I won! After saying goodbye to the frog, I took some time to think about what to do next. I could stay at the park and look around for more things to do, but I really wanted to find other places to go before I had to go back to my family. Soon, I was back out of the park and walking again.

I kept walking for a while, and I was not finding anything. Suddenly, I saw a big red building right in front of me, and had no idea what it was! Then, I realized it was a barn, and it was a part of a giant farm. Quickly, I ran over to it, because I knew a farm was the best place to find animals.

I walked into the barn through the giant red door, and right away, it was like I stepped into a zoo. Everywhere I looked, there were animals!

The first animal I saw was a huge horse, and she was very nice. She offered me water, and even gave me a tour of the entire barn. The horse was the kindest animal I met during my adventure!

"Have you been running all around?

You're making that panting sound!

There is some water right near the hen,

And to the left is the pig pen!

There are some cows further back,

And outside you'll hear ducks quack!"

-Elle the Horse

I explored the rest of the barn with her help, and then went outside. The one animal that I wanted to see but did not was a cat, but then something exciting happened. It was similar to when I got scared by the frog, but this time, it was a cat that made me afraid!

She was just waiting for me right outside the barn door. Her name was Kara, and she was the cutest cat I had ever seen! I went and talked to her for a moment next to the barn.

"I'm just a tiny, little cat,

How were you afraid of that?

I'm glad you came and met the horse,

She is very nice of course!

Don't forget to come again,

We'll be waiting until then!"

-Kara the Cat

I left the farm and all of the animals, and then I started walking back to the beach. The fish said that I needed to be back by four o'clock, and the sun was starting to go down, so I knew it was getting late!

I had met so many nice animals on my wonderful adventure. Little did I know, there were still more animals that I was going to see! As I ran to the beach, I saw something flying right in front of me. Soon, I realized it was a bird, flying right toward me. I thought that this bird wanted to play with me, but I was completely wrong!

This was the meanest bird I had ever seen. He flew really fast and was really scary. The bird had trapped me and was not letting me go! Even though he said he wanted to be friends, I knew that he was evil!

"Oh my little dog named Max,

Come and stay, you can relax!

Forever you and I will play,

You will stay here everyday!

There really is no way to leave,

At least that is what I believe!"

-Larry the Bird